W9-BOF-852

Lili Backstage

Rachel Isadora

PUFFIN BOOKS

For my mother

PUFFIN BOOKS
Published by the Penguin Group
Penguin Putnam Books for Young Readers, 345 Hudson Street, New York, New York 10014, U.S.A.
Penguin Books Ltd, 27 Wrights Lane, London W8 5TZ, England
Penguin Books Australia Ltd, Ringwood, Victoria, Australia
Penguin Books Canada Ltd, 10 Alcorn Avenue, Toronto, Ontario, Canada M4V 3B2
Penguin Books (N.Z.) Ltd, 182-190 Wairau Road, Auckland 10, New Zealand

Penguin Books Ltd, Registered Offices: Harmondsworth, Middlesex, England

First published in the United States by G. P. Putnam's Sons, a division of The Putnam & Grosset Group, 1997
Published in Puffin Books, a member of Penguin Putnam Books for Young Readers, 1999

1 3 5 7 9 10 8 6 4 2

Copyright © Rachel Isadora, 1997
All rights reserved

THE LIBRARY OF CONGRESS HAS CATALOGED THE G. P. PUTNAM'S SONS EDITION AS FOLLOWS:
Isadora, Rachel.
Lili backstage/Rachel Isadora. p. cm.
Summary: As she looks for her grandfather backstage, Lili sees some of
the different people involved in putting on a ballet performance.
[1. Ballet companies—Fiction. 2. Grandfathers—Fiction.] I. Title.
PZ7.1763Lj 1997 [E]—dc20 96-16361 CIP AC
ISBN 0-399-23025-4

This edition ISBN 0-698-11793-X

Printed in the United States of America

Except in the United States of America, this book is sold subject to the condition that it shall not,
by way of trade or otherwise, be lent, re-sold, hired out, or otherwise circulated without the publisher's
prior consent in any form of binding or cover other than that in which it is published and without
a similar condition including this condition being imposed on the subsequent purchaser.

Note to the Reader

The theater backstage is a world unto itself. It can be as colorful and as exciting as any performance. There are many more people contributing to a ballet production than there are dancers performing on stage.

Stagehands, costume designers, scenic artists, lighting technicians, musicians, and stage managers are just some of the people who make it possible for the show to go on.

I hope someday you get the opportunity to visit this very special place.

Rachel Isadora

Every Friday, Lili's mother picks her up after ballet class and they go home for dinner. But tonight, Lili's going to eat at the theater. "Have fun," her mother tells her.

First, Lili goes backstage and says hello to Harry, the guard.

"Hi, Lili! I bet I know who you're looking for. Why don't you check the rehearsal room."

Lili takes the elevator to the third floor and looks into the orchestra rehearsal studio. But it's empty. "How do they know which music stand is theirs?" Lili whispers and giggles.

She decides to look on the second floor, and on her way she sees some of the dancers in the ballet company rehearsing. She'd like to stay and watch, but today she doesn't have enough time.

She goes on past an open door.
"Hi," says Tony, the stage manager.
"Wow!" Lili says. "We are so high above the stage."
"I must check the scenery from up here, and then I have to change thirty lightbulbs," he tells her.

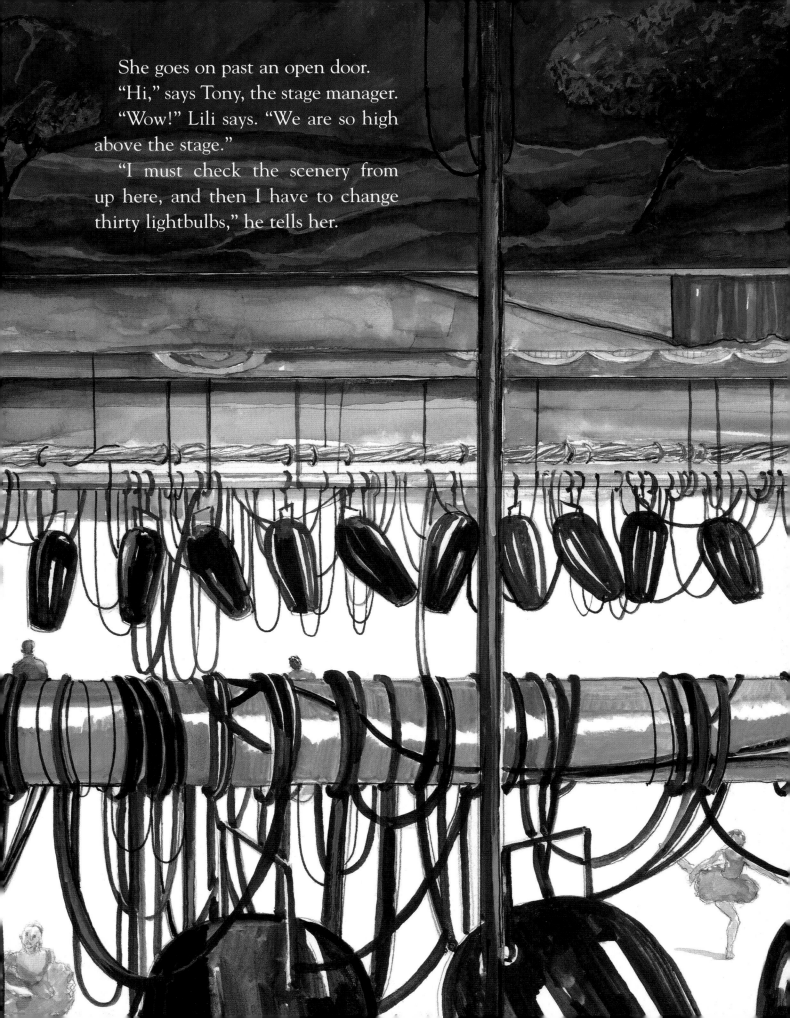

foundation stick

powder

mascara

from "The Sleeping Beauty"

Lilac Fairy

Court Dancer

Little Red Riding Hood

Lili goes down the stairs. When she walks past the makeup room she pauses to watch Cecilia put on her makeup for the Lilac Fairy. Some dancers take ten minutes to put on their makeup and some

eyeshadow

lipstick

blush

Bluebird

Carabosse

Queen

dancers take more than an hour. Dancers learn to apply heavy, dramatic makeup so they can be seen from the last rows in the audience.

Then, she walks past the wig room, where hats and head masks are also stored.

"Those would be great for Halloween," Lili says to herself and laughs.

On her way through the costume room, Lili waves to Margaret, the wardrobe mistress. She sees some of the younger students from her ballet school and remembers when she danced in *The Sleeping Beauty* last year. Now she's too big for the costume.

She goes to the canteen to look around.

"Hi, Lili," says Gabrielle, Lili's favorite ballerina.

"Are you dancing tonight?" Lili asks.

"Yes," says Gabrielle. "But I always like to come here to relax before a performance."

Some company members attend regular school and have homework to do.

These company members
are good friends and have
a lot to talk about.

Some of the
younger dancers
eat a snack.

Lili wishes Gabrielle good luck, then goes downstairs, under the stage. "This is spooky," Lili says to herself. "I wouldn't want to come down here to get my instrument."

She quickly goes up the stairs and looks in the prop room. "This is wild!" she exclaims, looking at all the props for the performances the company will dance throughout the year.

"One hour to curtain," Lili hears Tony announce over the speakers. She hurries to the stage. Suddenly she stops. She hears a baritone horn.

Lili steps in front of the curtain. "There you are, Grandpa! I've been looking all over for you!"

"I went to get us dinner. I hope you like pepperoni pizza," Grandpa Max says, smiling.

Max and Lili eat sitting in the orchestra pit. Then, Lili hurries backstage because tonight she's going to watch the performance from the wings.

Every time she hears the
baritone horn, she smiles.

When the performance ends and the curtain goes down, Lili meets her Grandpa Max in the orchestra pit.

"You were great, Grandpa!"

"Someday, Lili, you'll be dancing on stage and I'll be playing for *you!*"

"And *then* we can have pepperoni pizza every night!" Lili says, and gives Grandpa Max a big hug.